Color & Cook

HALLOWEEN

MONICA WELLINGTON

DOVER PUBLICATIONS, INC.
MINEOLA, NEW YORK

For Lydia, Phebe and Helen,
who have spent many happy Halloweens together

Note

Is Halloween one of your favorite holidays? Then you'll have lots of fun with this color-and-cook book! Read about how Molly and Jack are getting ready for their Halloween party: making invitations and decorating, sewing costumes, and preparing delicious treats, such as pumpkin cupcakes and goblin ice cream frosties. You will learn how to make them, too! Finally, join them as they go trick-or-treating. Have your crayons and markers ready, because you can color in every page.

Bibliographical Note

Color & Cook HALLOWEEN is a new work, first published by Dover Publications, Inc., in 2011.

International Standard Book Number

ISBN-13: 978-0-486-48106-7
ISBN-10: 0-486-48106-9

Manufactured in the United States by Courier Corporation
48106901
www.doverpublications.com

When the leaves turn pretty colors and the wind brings cooler weather,
it's time for Molly and Jack to get ready for Halloween.

1

They take a family drive to a farm and pick shiny red apples in the orchard.

They choose big orange pumpkins in the field.
They will load everything into the car to bring home.

Jack and Molly make jack-o-lanterns. They get a little bit of help with carving from Mom. Then they all carefully scoop out the seeds.

It is fun to make all kinds of faces.
They can be silly or scary. . . . Make up your own!

Now Molly and Jack make pumpkin cupcakes. First they mix the batter. The cupcakes bake in the oven. What a delicious, spicy smell!

6

Yellow

Vanilla

Red

Confectioners Sugar

They make colored frosting. They have a lot of fun ideas
for decorating their Halloween cupcakes.

Jack and Molly get ready to work on their Halloween costumes.
They get out their supplies.

scissors

ruler

needle and thread

pin cushion
with pins

buttons

fabric

measuring tape

GLUE

tape

beads

old clothes
to reuse

Ideas

notebook

ribbon

yarn

fabric markers

sequins

pipe cleaners

Yellow Blue Red

brush and paints

Can you find all of these sewing and craft items in the picture?

9

Back in the kitchen, Molly and Jack are making caramel apples.
Mom helps them melt the caramels.

10

Next, they make wormy, spidery SURPRISE popcorn balls.

Molly and Jack are planning a Halloween party.
They make invitations and decorations.

Can you help finish the decorations and color them in?

They cook some more Halloween recipes.

They are making jellied eyeballs and green slime punch!

It's time to cast a spell on their house, inside and . . .

. . . outside.

Book of Spells

Magic

fabBOOlous

Bloodshot Eyeballs

Creepy Bats

Slimy Slugs and Worms

Ancient Mummy

Screechy

Carved Pumpkins

Witch's Brew

Haunted Graveyard

Their haunted house is ready for Halloween.

Crawly Spider

Sneaky Mice

Weird Monster

Black Cat

Spooky Ghost

Scary Witch

Trick or Treat

R.I.P.

Bony Skeleton

Enter at your peril!

Molly dresses up as a witch. Her wig makes her look so different!
Her hat tops it all off.

Jack dresses up as a pirate, complete with a treasure map.
They are ready for Halloween!

Their friends arrive. Everyone is disguised in amazing costumes.
They can't wait to try Molly and Jack's Halloween treats.

22

And Mom has made another surprise: goblin ice cream frosties!
Inside the scooped-out oranges is delicious ice cream.

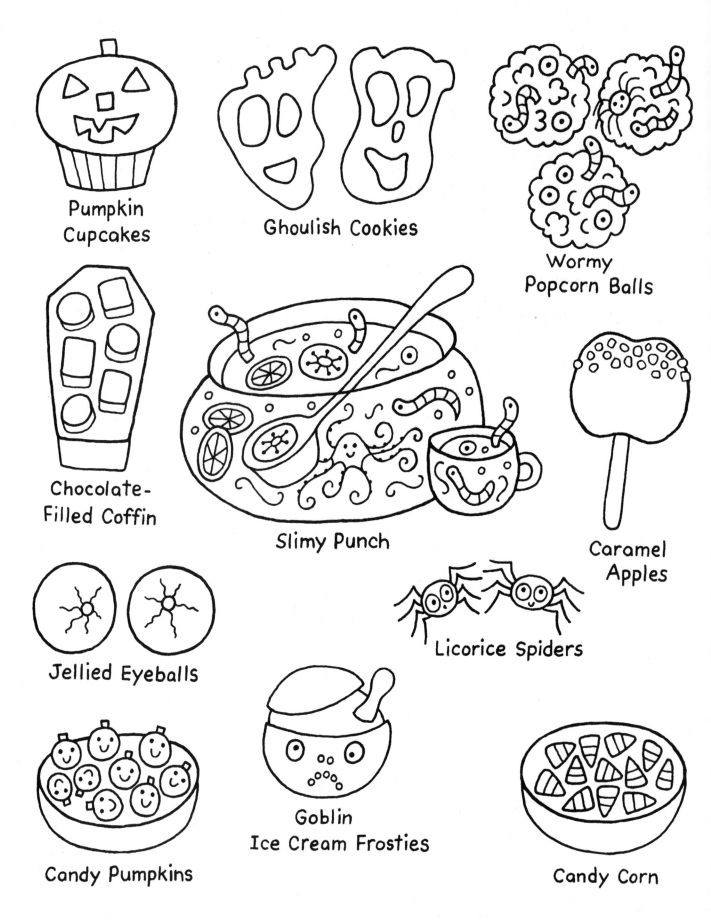

Pumpkin
Cupcakes

Ghoulish Cookies

Wormy
Popcorn Balls

Chocolate-
Filled Coffin

Slimy Punch

Caramel
Apples

Jellied Eyeballs

Licorice Spiders

Goblin
Ice Cream Frosties

Candy Pumpkins

Candy Corn

Some of the treats are gross or yucky or even scary, but all are yummy!
Can you find all of these treats in the picture?

"Bone Appetite," says the skeleton!

Hurrah—now it is time to go trick-or-treating.

Happy Halloween!

Recipes

Pumpkin Cupcakes

(Makes 12 cupcakes)

1 cup sugar
1/3 cup butter or oil
1 teaspoon vanilla extract
2 eggs
1 cup canned pumpkin
1²/3 cups flour

1/2 teaspoon salt
1 teaspoon baking soda
1/4 teaspoon baking powder
1 teaspoon cinnamon
1/4 teaspoon nutmeg
1/3 cup water

1. Preheat oven to 350 degrees.
2. Blend together sugar, butter and vanilla extract.
3. Add eggs and water and beat well.
4. Stir in pumpkin.
5. In another bowl, combine the flour, salt, baking powder, baking soda, cinnamon and nutmeg.
6. Add the flour mixture to the pumpkin mixture and blend until moistened. Batter will be a bit lumpy.
7. Place paper baking cups into muffin tray and fill with batter until each cup is about three-quarters full.
8. Bake for 19–21 minutes, or until golden brown or toothpick inserted into cupcake comes out clean.
9. Cool before icing with Cream Cheese Frosting.

Cream Cheese Frosting

1/3 of 8 oz. package of cream cheese
1 tablespoon softened butter
1/2 teaspoon vanilla extract
1 cup confectioners sugar

1. With an electric mixer, beat cream cheese and butter until well blended.
2. Add vanilla extract and beat in.
3. Gradually add sugar, and beat until smooth and slightly fluffy.
4. Add a couple of drops of yellow and red food dye if you want to make festive orange cupcakes for Halloween.

Note: Children should always have the assistance of an adult for help and safety.

Goblin Ice Cream Frosties

(Makes 6)

6 medium oranges   whole cloves
12 licorice (or fruit) soft candy drops
1 quart ice cream or sherbet of your choice
(try green: lime, pistachio, mint...)

1. Cut off a small slice of peel from the bottom of each orange to make it stand firmly.
2. For the hat, cut off a bigger slice from the top. With a spoon, scoop out the fruit from each orange.
3. Stick on candy for eyes, holding them in place with toothpicks. Insert whole cloves to form nose and mouth.
4. Fill each orange with ice cream, with extra above rim. Put the hats on top of each orange.
5. Place them in the freezer until serving time.

Wormy Popcorn Balls

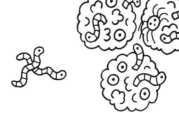

(Makes 10-12 popcorn balls)

8 cups popped popcorn
2 tablespoons butter
4 cups miniature marshmallows
chewy fruit-flavored worm-shaped gummies

1. Pop the popcorn and place it in a large buttered bowl.
2. In a saucepan over medium/low heat, melt the butter. Add the marshmallows and stir until they are melted.
3. Pour the marshmallow mixture slowly over the popcorn and stir gently to coat.
4. With buttered hands, take a handful of popcorn mixture (making sure it is not too hot), press 2 gummy worms into it and form a medium-sized ball (2½ inches to 3 inches in diameter). Let the worm heads stick out!

Caramel Apples

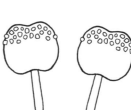

(Makes 6 apples)

6 apples on skewers
1 package of caramels

1. Wash and dry the apples and stick skewers in each apple.
2. Melt the caramels in a bowl in the microwave oven, or in a saucepan on the stove.
3. Working quickly, dip the apples into the hot caramel mixture. Using a knife, cover the top and any remaining areas with more hot caramel. Place the apples on foil paper to cool and harden.

Note: If the caramel mixture hardens while spreading, reheat it in the microwave or stove.
Optional: Immediately after dipping, roll the apples in finely chopped nuts.

Recipes

Jelllied Eyeballs

(Makes about 8)

1 packet of gelatin (in a yellow or light pink color)
An assortment of fruit (such as blueberries,
raspberries, some jumbo-sized green grapes and
strawberries, an apple, pear, kiwi, and/or can of lychees)
9 plastic cups for molds

1. Mash the strawberries with a fork to make a puree. Wash and prepare other fruits.
2. Assemble the fruit for the "eyeballs," and place each one, face down into the plastic cup/mold. For example, cut the grape in half, scoop out a little space and push in a blueberry "pupil." Cut the pear or apple across, into rings (cutting out the core in the center). Then fill the hole of a raspberry with a blueberry and put that in the center of the fruit ring. Drain the lychees, spoon strawberry puree into each hole and then plug it with a blueberry. Have fun!
3. Make the gelatin following the directions on the packet.
4. Pour into cups/molds, covering the fruit.
5. Put in refrigerator for at least 3 hours until set.
6. To unmold, dip each cup into very hot water for a few moments and then turn it over onto a serving plate.

Slime Punch

(serves 6)

1 cup sugar
½ cup boiling water
6 lemons
6 cups cold water
a few drops of green food coloring
slices of kiwi, lime and orange
an assortment of chewy worm and other-shaped gummies

1. To make the syrup, put sugar in heatproof bowl and add boiling water. Stir to dissolve sugar and set aside to cool.
2. Squeeze lemons for about 1 cup of juice.
3. In a punch bowl, combine the lemon juice, sugar syrup, cold water and a few drops of green food coloring.
4. Just before serving add fruit slices and assorted worm gummies. Serve chilled.

Note: Children should always have the assistance of an adult for help and safety.